A TIME TO WEAN

Written by Marlene Susan

Illustrated by Hayley Lowe

For Oliver and Coral—MS
For Elsinoor—HL

Corolishine Books: www.marlenesusan.com
ISBN # 9 78069 2054 9 87

The timing and process of weaning
is personal and different for everyone.
I hope you enjoy this book
when it's your child's time to wean.

When little kitten is first born,
mama cat nurses her snug and warm.

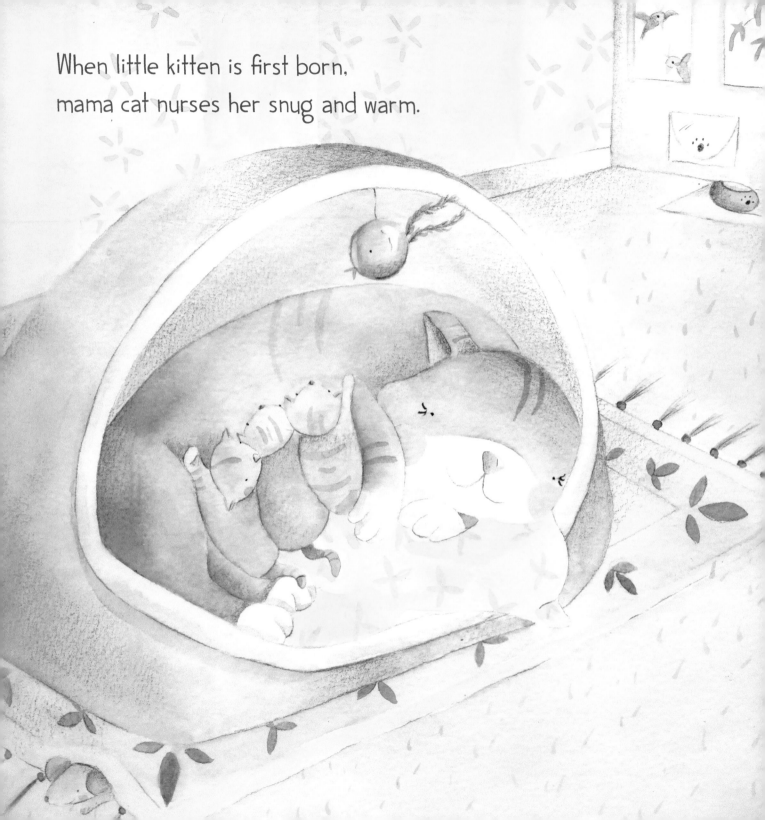

As kitten grows she nurses less,
and discovers new things she likes best.

Trees to climb,

mice on the run,

Hugs from mama, when day is done.

When little piglet is first born,
mama pig nurses him snug and warm.

As piglet grows he nurses less,
and discovers new things he likes best.

Corn to munch,

muddy fun,

Hugs from mama, when day is done.

When little lamb is first born,
mama sheep nurses her snug and warm.

As lamb grows she nurses less,
and discovers new things
she likes best.

Rolling meadows,

sweet grass in sun,

Hugs from mama, when day is done.

When little cub is first born,
mama bear nurses him snug and warm.

As cub grows he nurses less
and discovers new things he likes best.

Moonlit snow,

fish by the ton,

Hugs from mama, when day is done.

When you my child were first born,
mama nursed you snug and warm.

Now you too can nurse less,
and discover new things you like best.
Now and forever my little one,
I always love you when day is done.

Author

Marlene Susan lives in northern California with her husband and their two children. It was weaning them which inspired her to write this book. She loves to write, garden, and dance in the sunshine.

For more info and books visit www.marlenesusan.com

Illustrator

Hayley Lowe is a British-Canadian illustrator who lives in Vancouver with her husband and daughter. Away from her studio you will find Hayley with a paint-splattered camera forest stomping, people watching, moon bathing and mountain gazing.

Hayley and her daughter Elsinoor experienced the Time to Wean journey while working on this book, making it extra special!

For more info visit www.hayleylowe.com

Thank you

Thank you to all the people who were kind enough to help get this book made.

A very special thank you to the following for their extra generous contribution:

Danielle, Dawn, Doug, Gilden, Gonzalo, Howard, James, Jane, Jen, Jerry, Kris, Lori, Maggie, Margot, Moni, Nicole, Paul, Rae, Rachel, Sara, Seth, Steve, Timara, Tom, Vista

Love & thanks to JT

Printed in the USA
CPSIA information can be obtained
at www.ICGtesting.com
LVHW062114280324
775752LV00002B/66